Made in the USA
Monee, IL
16 December 2023

This BOOK is PERFECT!

By Ron Keres

Artwork by Arthur Lin

for Finley & Avery- R.K.
for my Perfect Family- A.L.

special thanks to Miss Jill

This BOOK is PERFECT!

By Ron Keres

Artwork by Arthur Lin

Oh, hello there.

I'm Finn the FROG and THIS, my friend, is the CLEANEST book you will ever see!

Some even say that it's **PERFECT**, but I don't really like to brag.

I know, I know. Most frogs are **SLIMY** and **DIRTY**. But not me. No way. You see, I am the tidiest frog you will ever meet.

I think you're going to be quite impressed with what you are about to see.

Now then, shall we begin?
Go on. Turn the page.

AHHHHH!

What is on your fingers?!
Are you eating **CHEESY PUFFS**
while reading **MY** book??

What are you thinking!?
You can't eat cheesy puffs
while reading this book! Wipe
your hands and put that
snack away **RIGHT NOW!!**

Whew, that's better. A little elbow grease goes a long way when keeping things neat, you know.

And after all, it could have been worse. It could have been—

GRAPE JUICE!

Are you kidding me?
Sticky, drippy grape juice
all over my **PERFECT** pages?

Listen, kid. If there is anything you've got to know in life, it's this: grape juice **ALWAYS** stains!

These pages are supposed to be white, not **PURPLE!** This is not good, kid. Not Good!

DRAT! This mop is worthless against such a mess! First the fingerprints, now the grape juice. I swear, this day couldn't get any—

This is a nightmare. It has to be.
Any minute now I'm going to wake
up and find out that there
is not **GUM** stuck on my page!
It will be fine. Really.

Any . . . minute . . . now.
Wake up, Finn. Wake up **NOW!**

It's not working. I don't think I'm dreaming.

Breathe, Finn, breathe. There must be something I can use to get that sticky thing off my book?

MAYDAY! MAYDAY! This is not a drill. I repeat, this is not a drill. My page is **RIPPING!**

This is a disaster! I was so excited to show you my book, but now it is ruined forever!

Ugh. I just want this all to be over. Maybe you should just close the book and end my misery.

WAIT! Don't close the book. Do you see what I see? This mess is attracting flies! Don't you know those tiny troublemakers throw up every time they land?

YUCK! Even the thought of fly **BARF** on my book is making me queasy.

Shoo, fly! Shoo! Go away!

Oh, no. That useless fly just landed on my book!
Think, Finn, think. How does one get rid of flies??

Hmmm. I wonder if my vacuum
has a turbo mode for sucking up flies?

NO! Don't smash it, kid. Do you have any idea the kind of mess that would leave behind? I mean, all the guts and other oozy stuff that comes out of a fly? Not on **MY** book!

There's got to be another way.

Me? Why are you looking at me?
What do you expect me to do?!

Oooooh. Right.

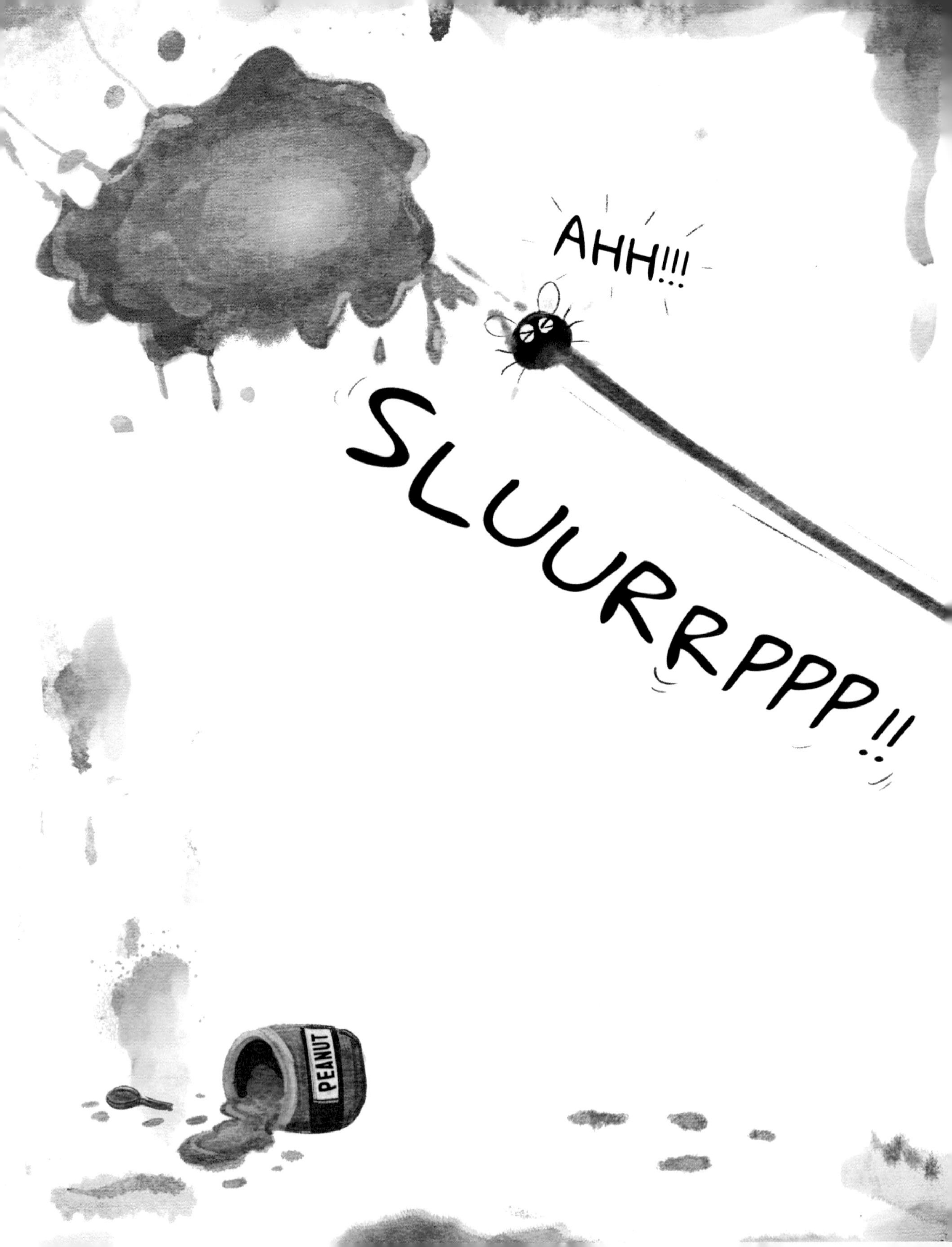
AHH!!!
SLUURRPPP!!
PEANUT

Mmmmm! **DEE-LISH!** I almost forgot how good those things taste!
You know, I still believe cleanliness is the best policy, but maybe this mess wasn't so terrible after all.

Come to think of it, without your help,
I never would have gotten these
tasty snacks! And besides, if I
can't live with the mess . . .

I can always turn the page!

THiS BOOK iS on
FIRE!
By Ron Keres
Artwork by Arthur Lin

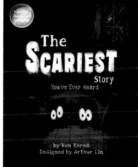
The
SCARIEST
Story
You've Ever Heard
by Ron Keres
Designed by Arthur Lin

For free downloadable
coloring sheets, please
visit ronkeres.com or scan
the code with your phone.

Enjoyed this book? Please leave a review!

Made in the USA
Monee, IL
16 December 2023

49689887R00021